S

To Len, who is not grumpy, either (honest!)
— S.S.

For Mel, who puts up with me when I'm grumpy and makes
me laugh when I need it most!
— C.P.

tiger tales
5 River Road, Suite 128, Wilton, CT 06897
Published in the United States 2019
Originally published in Great Britain 2019
by Little Tiger Press Ltd.
Text copyright © 2019 Steve Smallman
Illustrations copyright © 2019 Caroline Pedler
ISBN-13: 978-1-68010-130-0
ISBN-10: 1-68010-130-7
Printed in China
LTP/1400/2404/0918
10 9 8 7 6 5 4 3 2 1

For more insight and activities, visit us at www.tigertalesbooks.com

I'M NOT GRUMPY!

by Steve Smallman • Illustrated by Caroline Pedler

tiger tales

Mouse was in a grumpy mood.
He woke up to find that the door to his oak tree
was blocked by A BIG, FURRY BOTTOM!
"THAT'S JUST WHAT I NEED!" he grumbled,
climbing out the window to see
what was going on.

Then **SPLASH!** a drop of water landed on Mouse's nose.
"RAIN!" he grumbled. "THAT'S JUST WHAT I NEED!"

But it wasn't a raindrop.
It was a teardrop from a very sad little badger.

"WHERE'S MY MOMMY?" she wailed.
"I don't know!" squeaked Mouse.
"But I'll help you if you
STOP CRYING!"
Little Badger sniffed.
Then she took Mouse's paw,
and off they went.

They hadn't gone far when a butterfly fluttered past.
"PRETTY!" squealed Little Badger, galloping after it.
"STOP!" squeaked Mouse.

But when Little Badger did, Mouse was completely lost.
"THAT'S JUST WHAT I NEED!" he groaned.

"Hello," said a little voice.

"Aren't you that grumpy mouse who lives in the old oak tree?"

"I'M NOT GRUMPY!" said Mouse grumpily.

"I'm trying to get this little badger back to her mommy."

"How kind!" said Squirrel. "My friend will know
where the Badgers live. Come on!"

"Hello, Squirrel," hooted Owl.
"What a dear little badger! Oh, and you've brought lunch."
"I AM NOT LUNCH!" sputtered Mouse.
"Indeed," nodded Owl. "You're that grumpy mouse.
I don't eat grumpy mice. They're much too sour."
"Actually," said Squirrel, "he's trying to get
Little Badger back home to her mommy!"

"Then follow me," smiled Owl. "The forest is a dangerous place after dark, so we'd better get going!"

Everyone followed Owl deeper
into the forest when suddenly . . .

SPLOSH!

a drop of water landed on Mouse's nose.
"Oh, please don't start crying again!"
grumbled Mouse.

But it wasn't a teardrop.
It was a raindrop!

"THAT'S JUST WHAT I NEED!"

Mouse huffed as it started to pour.

"We must keep Little Badger dry," said Owl.

"Soggy badgers catch colds."

"Oh, no!" gasped Mouse.

"Does anyone have an umbrella?"

"You're welcome to take
shelter under my tummy,"
said a big brown bear.
"But what is the grumpy mouse
doing out here with
Little Badger?"

"He's trying to get her home,"
said Squirrel quickly.
"What a kind friend!" smiled Bear.
Mouse blushed. He'd never been
called a friend before.

When the rain stopped, Bear pointed them in the right direction.
"And you'd better hurry," he said. "It's getting late!"

On they trudged through
the darkening forest. Little Badger yawned.
"She's tired!" said Squirrel as shadows
stretched across their path.
"Well, it's way past her bedtime,"
agreed Owl.

"I KNOW!" cried Mouse.

"She's TIRED, AND HUNGRY,
AND SCARED. AND SHE NEEDS HER MOMMY,
AND IT'S GETTING DARK, AND . . .
I don't know what to do!" he sobbed.

"There, there," said Squirrel.
Owl spread his wings. "I know what you need."
"HUG!" cheered Little Badger.

Mouse felt funny. Being a bit of a grumpy mouse,
he didn't get very many cuddles.

Suddenly, there was a flash of gray in the bushes.
"Mommy?" called Little Badger hopefully.
But it wasn't Mommy Badger. It was . . .

. . . a WOLF!

He swaggered over, licking his lips.

"Look what we have here!" the wolf snickered.
"A squirrel for starters, a badger
and an owl for the main course,
and a mouse for dessert!"

"I AM NOT DESSERT!"
shouted Mouse angrily.

"AND YOU CAN'T EAT MY FRIENDS!"
"Says who?" sneered the wolf.

"ME!"
shouted Mouse.

"AND ME!"
shouted Owl.

"AND ME!"
shouted Squirrel.

"AND ME!"

shouted Mommy Badger.

The wolf took one look at her angry eyes and ran away.

Mommy Badger hugged Little Badger tightly. "Thank you all for bringing her home!"

"It was Mouse's idea," said Squirrel.
"Well, thank you, Mr.— wait a minute,"
said Mommy Badger. "Aren't you the grumpy mouse
who lives in the oak tree?"

"For the last time," huffed Mouse,
"I'M NOT GRUMPY . . .

"... at least, not anymore!"
And for the first time in a long time, Mouse smiled.

"Because now I have friends," he said.
"And friends—well, THAT'S JUST WHAT I NEED!"